D1103343

Fergus the Sea Dog

For Rebecca and new baby granddaughter Molly

MYRIAD BOOKS LIMITED
35 Bishopsthorpe Road, London SE26 4PA

First published in 2004 by
PICCADILLY PRESS LIMITED
5 Castle Road, London NW1 8PR
www.piccadillypress.co.uk

Text and illustrations copyright © Tony Maddox 2004

Tony Maddox has asserted his right to be identified as the author and illustrator
of this work in accordance with the Copyright, Designs and Patents Act, 1988.

All rights reserved. No part of this publication may be reproduced, stored in a
retrieval system, or transmitted, in any form or by any means electronic, mechanical,
photocopying or otherwise, without prior permission of the copyright owner.

ISBN 1 905606 94 X
EAN 9 781905 606 948

Cover design by Tony Maddox and Fielding Design
Text design by Tony Maddox and Louise Millar

Printed in China

ROTHERHAM LIBRARY &
INFORMATION SERVICES

PB
B49 030 4883
OES 426724

Fergus the Sea Dog

Tony Maddox

MYRIAD BOOKS LIMITED

Fergus was excited.
This was his first holiday at the seaside.
"WOOF WOOF WOOF!" he barked as he
rushed to explore the beach with Farmer Bob.

There were so many things to do!

He found hidden rock
pools, where small
fish darted in and
out of the weeds and
baby crabs scuttled
to hide under stones.

He explored dark, damp
caves with strange, scary echoes.

He played games with Farmer Bob,
who threw sticks in the water
for him to fetch.

The next morning, Fergus woke early and went down to the beach on his own.
He was busy digging a hole in the sand when he noticed another dog watching him.

The dog looked friendly, so Fergus
wagged his tail.

The dog
wagged his tail too, and
they both knew they could be friends.

Fergus had a new friend to play with!

Off they went, chasing each other across
the beach . . . "WOOF WOOF WOOF!"
and around the rocks . . .

"WOOF WOOF WOOF!"

Splashing through the waves . . .
"WOOF WOOF WOOF!"
and scaring the seagulls . . .
"WOOF WOOF WOOF!"

After they had played for a while, Fergus's new
friend ran up on to the long stone pier.
"WOOF WOOF!" he called over his shoulder.
He wanted Fergus to follow him . . .

A small fishing boat was
moored at the end of the pier.
The Captain was just about
to set sail.
"Come on, Salty!" he
called out. "We don't want
to miss the tide! Is your
friend coming too?"

This was going to be
an adventure!

Fergus and Salty lay on the deck as the Captain checked his crab pots. Sunlight sparkled on the lazy waves and seagulls swooped and swirled overhead.
"This is the life for me!" thought Fergus.
"So peaceful, and no farm animals to bother me. I should be a sea dog just like Salty!"

The Captain was pleased with his catch. "There's a beauty!" he said proudly, holding up one of the crabs. "Don't get too close . . . unless you want your noses nipped!" he chuckled.

Suddenly Fergus's ears shot up.
He thought he'd heard a
strange noise coming
from the sea.

"Aaarf
Aaarf!"

There it was again! The same frightened cry.
"WOOF!" he said to Salty.
They crept to the side
of the boat to see what
was making the
noise, and
saw . . .

. . . a small baby seal!

The Captain came over to see.
"Looks like this little pup's in trouble!" he said.
"It probably swam out too far and is too tired to swim back. Better take it back to its family."

Gently, he lifted the baby seal out of the water and on to the deck.

"Aaarf!" said the baby seal.
"WOOF!" said Fergus.

When the baby seal was safely back with its family, the Captain began putting on his sou'wester. "I can smell rain!" he said. "Better get home quick!"

Moments later, the sky darkened and raindrops began pattering on the wheelhouse roof where Fergus and Salty were sheltering.

Before long, the little fishing boat was
being tossed up and down on giant
waves, and heavy rain beat against
the wheelhouse windows.
Fergus huddled up to Salty as the
Captain struggled to steer the boat.
Everything seemed to be turning
upside down and Fergus was
beginning to feel very sick.
"I wish I was back on the
farm!" he groaned.

After what seemed like a very long time, they were safely back in the harbour. Fergus staggered up the steps on wobbly legs, then said goodbye to Salty and the Captain.

Cold and wet, he made his way
home to the holiday cottage.
He was pleased to see Farmer Bob
waiting at the garden gate.

Fergus snuggled into his comfy basket and closed his eyes. He thought about all the animals back at the farm. He couldn't wait to tell them of the things he'd done.

"Perhaps being a farm dog isn't so bad after all," he thought as he drifted off to sleep.